Last Chance Romance

A Comedy

by

Sam Bobrick

SAMUEL FRENCH

FOUNDED 1830

NEW YORK HOLLYWOOD LONDON TORONTO

SAMUELFRENCH.COM

ISBN 978-0-573-66265-2   Printed in U.S.A.   #14732

IMPORTANT BILLING AND CREDIT REQUIREMENTS

CHARACTERS

(In Order of Appearance)

LEONARD SHANK – A man in his early forties

MYRA WITZER – A woman in her late thirties

FLORENCE WITZER – Myra's seventy year-old mother

UNCLE FRED – Myra's sixty year-old Uncle

GLORIA FOSSBERG – Myra's therapist, in her late thirties or early forties.

NURSE SYLVIA – Leonard's nurse

WAITER – A man or woman

HOWARD – A man in his mid-forties

NOTE: Outside of Myra and Leonard, all other parts can be doubled up at the director's discretion, played by only two other actors, a man and woman.

ACT I

Scene 1

THE SET: *The main set is the living/dining room of Leonard Shank's apartment. It is modestly and unspectacularly furnished. The front door is at Upstage Right Center, a living room window at Upstage Left Center. A door leading to the bedroom is at Upstage Left. An open doorway leading to the kitchen is at Stage Right. A small dining table with several chairs are at Stage Right. A side table for the cordless phone is at Upstage Right. A sofa and coffee table are at Center Stage Left. Two small arm chairs and side tables are at an angle next to the sofa. A few other accessory pieces, a lamp, lamp table, several wall pictures, etc., are scattered around where necessary. When indicated in the play, the set will go dark and we will use lit downstage areas.*

TIME: *The Present. Early evening*

PLACE: *Leonard Shank's apartment.*

AT RISE: *The set is dark. The area around Leonard's dining room table lights up revealing a hesitant* **LEONARD SHANK**, *a man in his early forties, wearing suit pants and a dress shirt, standing near the table, dialing his cordless phone. His suit jacket hangs over a chair. At this moment in time,* **LEONARD** *is very unsure of himself and during the conversation he fidgets about. In a corner, Downstage Left, an area lights up on a small table with a cordless phone. The phone is RINGING.* **MYRA WITZER**, *a woman in her late thirties, wearing a skirt and blouse, enters and picks up the phone. At this moment in time,* **MYRA** *is a no nonsense, impatient woman who needs others to get to the point quickly.*

MYRA. Hello.

LEONARD. Uh, yes. Uh..uh..uh..

MYRA. *(Impatient)* What?

LEONARD. Is this...Myra Witzer?

MYRA. Yes it is.

LEONARD. Good. My name is Leonard Shank. I got your number from a friend of my aunt who was sitting on a bus with one of your mother's neighbors and by coincidence our two names came up and they thought it might be a good idea if maybe we, uh...we uh, we...

MYRA. Meet?

LEONARD. Yes. Meet. I guess that's the right word for it, isn't it?

MYRA. I don't think there's any other word that puts it so clearly.

LEONARD. That's probably why it's used so often. Especially in cases like this.

MYRA. Uh huh. I was alerted you'd be calling.

LEONARD. Oh. Oh good.

MYRA. That was two years ago.

LEONARD. Yes. Well, I...I lost your number.

MYRA. No, you didn't.

LEONARD. No, you're right. I didn't. I uh...I was in a...a...a relationship.

MYRA. No, you weren't.

LEONARD. Yes, yes, you're right. I wasn't. The truth is I kept hoping I wouldn't have to resort to this.

MYRA. Bingo!

LEONARD. My life is hopeless. I've hit bottom.

MYRA. Keep going. You're doing great.

LEONARD. I can't seem to meet anyone.

MYRA. Your right on track and moving like a bandit.

LEONARD. I've tried dating services, joined singles clubs, went on line, nothing seemed to work.

MYRA. You're nearing the finishing line. The crowd is cheering.

LEONARD. I actually thought seriously about trying the gay way. I saw "Brokeback Mountain" four times.

MYRA. Tough break, Leonard. Your horse just had a coronary.

LEONARD. But I couldn't go that route. My taste in clothing seemed to discourage that option. So here I am.

MYRA. Yes, and frankly it sounds like not a moment too soon.

LEONARD. You uh...you sound wonderful.

MYRA. Yes, I know. Okay, moving on to round two, just what is it you do for a living, Leonard?

LEONARD. I work for the city. I'm in the elevator permits department.

MYRA. *(A bit disappointed)* Oh.

LEONARD. Are you okay with that? I mean it is a white collar job and financially I don't do badly at all.

MYRA. Well, quite honestly, I was really hoping for a professional, but I imagine you have good medical benefits and job security, right?

LEONARD. Yes. And the retirement package is excellent.

MYRA. Well, I guess that'll do.

LEONARD. What about you?

MYRA. I'm in between jobs now. I'm thinking about a career change.

LEONARD. Oh. Very good. What was it you were doing?

MYRA. I was a temp. It was great for a while but now I think it's time to zero in on something a little more substantial.

LEONARD. That seems wise.

MYRA. I'd like to find something where I can give back to the community.

LEONARD. How generous.

MYRA. Well, that's the way I am. Anyway, Leonard, I assume you'd like to get together.

LEONARD. Yes. Yes I would.

MYRA. You didn't ask me if I was available.

LEONARD. That's true. Are you available?

MYRA. As a matter of fact, I just broke up with someone.

LEONARD. No you didn't.

MYRA. I've been in Europe for the last two years.

LEONARD. No, you weren't.

MYRA. I'm at the end of my dating rope and I can't tell you how happy I am you called.

LEONARD. You're very easy to talk to Myra Witzer. I hardly feel nauseous at all. So tell me a little bit more about yourself.

MYRA. No. I'd rather not. You might be so overwhelmed by what you hear you most likely would not find the courage to call me again, which I think would be a big mistake, because just from this short conversation with you I sense that there definitely could be potential here and I believe it's best to meet face to face as soon as possible.

LEONARD. Face to face?

MYRA. Yes.

LEONARD. Isn't it a little early for that? Don't you think we need a few more phone calls, maybe an exchange of pictures, possibly a look at some medical records?

MYRA. Look, Leonard let's be totally above board about this and look at it rationally. You're how old?

LEONARD. Thirty-six.

MYRA. Keep going.

LEONARD. Forty-one. What about you?

MYRA. I'm thirty-two.

LEONARD. Keep going.

MYRA. Thirty-four.

LEONARD. One more time with a little bump.

MYRA. Thirty-eight.

LEONARD. Good girl.

MYRA. That was liberating. Anyway, we're both going

nowhere with relationships and it's obvious we are getting to the desperation point. Therefore, I think it's almost mandatory to make every effort to make this one work if at all possible.

LEONARD. Gosh, that sounds so sensible it's scary. I need to warn you, Myra, in some areas I'm a very shallow person. Even though we seem to have a rapport on the phone, there needs to be a strong physical attraction for me.

MYRA. No, there doesn't.

LEONARD. Yes, there does.

MYRA. No, there doesn't.

LEONARD. Yes, there does.

MYRA. Leonard, when was the last time you had sex?

LEONARD. Four years ago.

MYRA. No, there doesn't.

LEONARD. You may be right.

MYRA. Besides Leonard, quite often just hanging around someone long enough...well you adjust to their physical shortcomings whatever they are, and suddenly the magnetism of the sexuality just happens.

LEONARD. You've had that happen to you?

MYRA. No, but there's always a first time. Now, where should we meet?

LEONARD. Well, usually the first date is for coffee.

MYRA. I'm sorry. I don't drink coffee.

LEONARD. Oh? Well, I guess we could make it for lunch.

MYRA. Dinner would be better.

LEONARD. Dinner? That's a real commitment, isn't it?

MYRA. We'll split the check if that's what you're worried about.

LEONARD. Oh, no. I'm not worried about that at all.

MYRA. Oh, that's very generous of you, Leonard. Let's pick a moderately priced restaurant. How about La Bourgeoise on East 81st? I understand they have entrees under fifty dollars.

LEONARD. Pick again.

MYRA. Okay, then how about Manny's Deli on 34th street? They have wonderful salads and all the bread and pickles you want.

LEONARD. That sounds good. Pick a day and I'll be there.

MYRA. How about Tuesday?

LEONARD. That's tomorrow.

MYRA. Yes. That way if we really hit it off we'll be able to plan something for the weekend.

LEONARD. This weekend? Well, I might be busy this weekend.

MYRA. No, you're not.

LEONARD. Okay, Tuesday evening at seven.

MYRA. Perfect. See you then, Leonard.

LEONARD. Right, Myra.

(They hang up at the exact same time and then simultaneously to the audience.)

BOTH. *(With great hope)* Possibilities!

(BLACK OUT)

Scene 2

SET: The main set stays dark. LIGHTS UP Downstage Center where a semi-circular restaurant booth has been pushed in.

TIME: Tuesday evening.

PLACE: Manny's Deli. **MYRA**, *sits in the booth next to her mother,* **FLORENCE**, *who is asleep in the center seat.* **MYRA** *offers her mother the bread basket.*

MYRA. Would you like some more bread or pickles, Mother?

*(***FLORENCE*** doesn't answer her. She speaks a little louder.)*

More bread or pickles, mother?

FLORENCE. *(Waking up)* What?

MYRA. More bread or pickles?

FLORENCE. No. No thanks. I'll take them home with me when we leave.

*(***MYRA*** puts the dish down. She looks at her watch.)*

MYRA. He's seven minutes late. I hope he hasn't gotten cold feet.

FLORENCE. Think positive, Myra. Maybe he was killed in a traffic accident.

MYRA. I don't know why, but I have a good feeling about this one. There was something in his voice, a sense of desperation, a fear of maybe having to die alone.

FLORENCE. Your father had that.

MYRA. Really?

FLORENCE. Yes. It was a fear before we were married and then afterwards it became a preference.

MYRA. You're too hard on yourself.

FLORENCE. I've been told that. Maybe I will have some more bread.

(She begins buttering and eating her bread)

MYRA. *(Looks at watch)* He's eight minutes late. I'm really annoyed now. If he does show up I'm going to order dessert. It is so humiliating, being in the singles market at my age.

FLORENCE. It's your own fault. You waited too long. I always encouraged you to get married while you were in your twenties.

MYRA. You didn't encourage, you nagged.

FLORENCE. You should have listened to me. You had your looks then, your energy, your enthusiasm for life. Now you're in your late thirties and what have you got left?

MYRA. My mother.

FLORENCE. I'm not going to be around forever.

MYRA. I'm counting on that.

*(**LEONARD** approaches the table.)*

LEONARD. By any chance are you...waiting for someone?

MYRA. Leonard?

LEONARD. Yes. Myra?

FLORENCE. Yes. You're ten minutes late.

MYRA. I'm sure he has a good excuse. You have a good excuse, don't you Leonard?

LEONARD. I was actually right on time, but I was looking for someone sitting alone and, well, you're not sitting alone.

FLORENCE. I'm her mother.

MYRA. This is my mother.

LEONARD. Your mother. I...we...I mean in our conversation there was no mention of you bringing your mother.

FLORENCE. Surprise! Sit down Leonard and let's order. My stomach is starting to make gurgling sounds.

LEONARD. Uh...yes.

*(He realizes the only place for him to sit down is next to **FLORENCE**.)*

I guess I'll sit right here.

FLORENCE. Good choice.

MYRA. I hope you don't mind my bringing my mother. It's sort of a safety precaution.

LEONARD. Safety? You didn't think you could trust me?

MYRA. No, not that at all. The last time I left her home she set the kitchen on fire.

LEONARD. She lives with you?

MYRA. No.

LEONARD. Oh, good.

MYRA. I live with her.

LEONARD. You don't have your own place?

MYRA. Well, it didn't make sense. She has a two bedroom apartment and since the death of my father I didn't think it was good for her to be alone.

LEONARD. No, no. Of course not. When did your father die?

MYRA. When I was seven. He was hit by a train.

LEONARD. Oh, that must have been awful.

MYRA. Yes it was. Freak accident. It seemed his car got stuck in the crossing.

FLORENCE. I could have sued the railroad and been sitting pretty today, but that goddamn suicide note of his made it almost impossible.

MYRA. Look, Leonard, if my mother being here is going to be a problem for you, I will gladly pay her share of the dinner bill.

LEONARD. Oh, no, no. That's not the problem.

MYRA. Thank you. You're quite generous. I like that in a man.

FLORENCE. Can we order? I'm fucking starved.

LEONARD. Yes, yes of course.

FLORENCE. I'll have soup, a salad, a side of broccoli, the rib steak and a chocolate sundae for dessert.

MYRA. That sounds good. I think I'll have the same. How about you, Leonard?

LEONARD. I haven't seen the menu but I'm thinking in

terms of a grilled cheese.

MYRA. Level with me now, Leonard. You're not a vegetarian are you, because I have absolutely no luck with vegetarians.

LEONARD. No, no, I'm not. It's just that...well..

MYRA. Be honest, Leonard. It's important we keep this relationship open and honest.

LEONARD. Well, I've been listening to this guy on the radio who talks about dating and he said anytime you spend over fifty dollars on a date, you'd better be sure you're going to have sex.

MYRA. Really.

LEONARD. Really!

FLORENCE. Well, in that case I'll also have two orders of fries and a couple of Bloody Marys. And I thought tonight was going to be dull.

(**LEONARD** *and* **MYRA** *look at her.*)

(*BLACKOUT*)

Scene 3

TIME: *Later that evening.*

The stage is dark. The Downstage Left area lights up on Myra's land phone. **MYRA** *enters, picks up the phone and dials. Leonard's dining table area lights up. His phone begins to ring. After six rings,* **LEONARD** *enters the apartment and answers the phone. They are both wearing the same clothes they wore in the restaurant.*

LEONARD. Yes?

MYRA. Leonard, it's me, Myra. I was just wondering why you haven't called.

LEONARD. I just got home a few seconds ago.

MYRA. Yes, maybe so. But at the end of the evening you seemed so excited, I thought for sure you'd call as soon as you got home. We seemed to hit it off so well. Even my mother was impressed. She can't wait to see you again.

LEONARD. I'll bet.

MYRA. She thought that was so generous of you. Not only to pay for her meal but to pay for the food she ordered to take home.

LEONARD. Look, Myra. I'm not going to beat around the bush. I don't think the evening worked out well for me.

MYRA. You're joking?

LEONARD. No, no. I'm serious.

MYRA. Oh, my God. I feel awful.

LEONARD. No, no. It's not you Myra. It's just that, well, you live with your mother...

MYRA. Yes.

LEONARD. And well, I live with mine.

MYRA. No.

LEONARD. Yes. And coincidentally, she's also getting over the death of my father.

MYRA. Oh, that's too bad. When did he die?

LEONARD. Sadly to say, about six months ago.

MYRA. I'm so sorry. He wasn't hit by a train by any chance?

LEONARD. No, no. He was electrocuted.

MYRA. Oh, good. I mean I've heard it's so much better than being hit by a train. Electrocuted, huh?

LEONARD. Yes. In the State Prison.

MYRA. He was a murderer?

LEONARD. No. An electrician. He was working on the chair when things went wrong. I've been against the death penalty ever since. Anyway, I'm sorry things didn't work out for us but those are the breaks of the dating game.

MYRA. No, no, wait, Leonard. Things actually worked out better than you think.

LEONARD. I don't understand.

MYRA. It's so obvious, Leonard. You live with your mother in one apartment and I live with mine in another. One of the problems is that reasonable apartments in the city are extremely hard to come by.

LEONARD. So?

MYRA. So what if we put them together?

LEONARD. Together.

MYRA. Yes. They live together in one apartment and we live together in the other. It's a win-win situation.

LEONARD. Wait a minute. Aren't you rushing things a little? I'm not sure you and I are even compatible.

MYRA. We can work that part out later. This is wonderful. This is that rare window of opportunity I've heard so much about. Oh, Leonard, this is the closest I've ever come to true happiness.

LEONARD. Really? I'm sorry to hear that.

MYRA. I'm so excited. Now, when can the four of us get together to work things out?

LEONARD. Well...well, first I'd have to break the news to my mother.

MYRA. Please, go right ahead. Tell her. I'll wait on the phone.

LEONARD. I...I can't tell her. Not right now. She's...She's still in a coma.

MYRA. A what?

LEONARD. A coma. She was hit by a bus last week and hasn't come around yet.

MYRA. A bus. Your mother was hit by a bus, my father was hit by a train. The karma, as well as the large amount of death between us, is unbelievable.

LEONARD. It seems that way, doesn't it?

MYRA. Definitely. So then what I'm hearing Leonard is that for all practical purposes you have the apartment all to your self. Oh, my gosh. The perks keep pouring in.

LEONARD. Well, no, not exactly. I mean I don't exactly have the apartment to myself. See, there wasn't room at the hospital for my mother so we set up things in her bedroom. The good news is that she can regain consciousness any minute. In fact, I think I hear her mumbling.

(Holds phone away and mumbles. Then gets back on phone)

Hear that? Maybe I'd better go in and take a look.

MYRA. Leonard, I think you're lying to me.

LEONARD. No, I'm not.

MYRA. Yes, you are!

LEONARD. I swear I'm not. I swear on my mother's grave. Ooops.

MYRA. Your mother's grave?

LEONARD. It's just an expression. I use it all the time.

MYRA. Why did you lie to me, Leonard?

LEONARD. Well, it just seemed easier that way.

MYRA. Your mother is dead?

LEONARD. Well, uh...

MYRA. You wonderful man. You wonderful, wonderful man.

LEONARD. Really?

MYRA. You didn't want to hurt my feelings, did you?

LEONARD. I didn't? No, I didn't.

MYRA. Of course not. You didn't want to tell me that this evening didn't work out as well as you hoped it would.

LEONARD. Well, actually, I did tell you that.

MYRA. Oh, my God, Leonard. You are a diamond among stones. You made all this up to spare my feelings, to keep from telling me that you didn't particularly care for me.

LEONARD. Well, I...

MYRA. Oh, my God. Never! Never, never, never did I dare dream you would be as sensitive a person as you turned out to be. Especially, after you slapped my mother's hand when she tried to take the dill pickle from your plate.

LEONARD. She's an old woman. Salt isn't good for her.

MYRA. Okay, okay. I have the whole picture now, Leonard. You are a considerate, caring, beautiful man who just doesn't want to get involved.

LEONARD. Yes. Exactly. Not at this time anyway.

MYRA. It's the sex thing, isn't it? You're afraid of sex, aren't you?

LEONARD. No, no. Not at all.

MYRA. Are you sure? Four years without it can often cause severe damage.

LEONARD. I assure you there are no damages.

MYRA. It's a performance thing, isn't it? Of course. I should have sensed that earlier in the evening. If you don't use it, you lose it. You're worried you can't get it up, right, Leonard?

LEONARD. Not at all. Maybe I didn't have actual sex with a woman but men have other ways to handle things.

MYRA. You mean masturbation?

LEONARD. This conversation is getting a little personal, don't you think?

MYRA. Oh, get off it, Leonard. Masturbation is a very normal, natural thing. This may come as a shock to you but women also masturbate.

LEONARD. Yes, I've heard that and it's not at all a shock.

MYRA. Good. Where is your favorite place to do it? Mine is sitting on top of the clothes dryer with the machine going around and around in the dry cycle.

LEONARD. Oh, jeez.

MYRA. I bet yours is equally creative. I hear guys will do it anywhere. Libraries, roller coasters, hardware stores…

LEONARD. Oh, jeez.

MYRA. By any chance Leonard, is this conversation starting to make you hot, because I'm starting to feel a bit tingly myself. In fact, as we're talking I'm walking to the clothes dryer.

LEONARD. No, stop, please, don't.

MYRA. Did you ever have phone sex, Leonard? It's not quite like the real thing, but it's not too bad in a pinch. I think we may be having that right now.

LEONARD. I'm warning you, I'm going to hang up.

MYRA. Oh, come on, Leonard. After behaving as decently as you have you're entitled to something. Maybe you want me to come over? That's it, you want me to come over, don't you, Leonard? This conversation has gotten you hot and sticky. Well, that's okay with me because since we're both being so honest with each other, the fact is I'm so physically attracted to you, my body would know no limits, do you know what I mean?

LEONARD. Well, uh, define limits?

MYRA. I need to see you Leonard. I need to see you and give you a night you'll never forget.

LEONARD. I think I already had that.

MYRA. I'll grab a cab and be there in twenty minutes.

LEONARD. Look, I don't think that's the right thing to do.

MYRA. Don't argue with me, Leonard. The wheels are in motion. I have your address. I looked it up in the phone book. You're not unlisted. That's another sad sign.

LEONARD. Wait! What about your mother? You said you can't leave her alone.

MYRA. She'll be fine. I just need to put the bars up on her bed so she doesn't fall out. You're not going to be sorry, Leonard Shank. That I promise you.

LEONARD. Well, if you insist.

MYRA. You're excited now, aren't you?

LEONARD. Well, uh, sort of.

MYRA. See you in twenty, Leonard.

(She hangs up. LIGHTS GO OFF on MYRA. LEONARD stands a moment with the phone in his hands. A look of fear and confusion is on his face.)

LEONARD. She's a whack job, but sex is sex.

(BLACK OUT)

Scene 4

TIME: Even later that same night.

PLACE: Leonard's apartment.

The doorbell rings. **LEONARD**, *now wearing pajamas, slippers and a silk robe ENTERS from bedroom, crosses and opens the front door.* **MYRA** *stands there with* **UNCLE FRED**, *an elderly gentleman, in a suit and carrying a briefcase.*

MYRA. Hi sweetie.

(She enters, giving a confused **LEONARD** *a kiss.* **UNCLE FRED** *follows her in and closes the door.)*

LEONARD. Who...Who's this?

MYRA. My Uncle Fred.

UNCLE FRED. Nice to meet you, young man. My niece can't seem to stop talking about you.

LEONARD. Your Uncle Fred? I thought you were coming alone.

MYRA. I know, I know. I'm sorry. I can see a little disappointment on your face. But I've been thinking this over. I like you, Leonard, and I know you like me, otherwise why would you let me come over here so late at night. Right?

LEONARD. Well, I thought we were going to have uh...uh...

MYRA. Sex. Yes, I know and that will come, but the bottom line is well, I don't want to see you get hurt.

LEONARD. Hurt? Why will I get hurt?

MYRA. Uncle Fred is a lawyer, Leonard.

LEONARD. So?

MYRA. So for your own protection I think the sooner we start working on a prenuptial agreement the better.

LEONARD. Oh, jeez.

MYRA. I know it sounds a bit premature but this is for your own good. You just met me. You have no idea who I really am.

LEONARD. I have a wonderful idea who you are. You're a certified nut job.

UNCLE FRED. You've got a nice place here, Leonard. You apparently do very well. You can't believe some of the dead beats my niece has brought around.

MYRA. Listen to me, Leonard. This evening could be a one night stand and that would be fine. But just in case it ends up to be something more...

LEONARD. Trust me. I had no intentions of it being anything more.

MYRA. And I respect that. But what if it isn't? What if you find you've fallen madly in love with me?

LEONARD. I'll immediately put myself in an institution.

MYRA. Madly, hopelessly in love with me. We get married, partake in all the early joy and bliss that comes with the territory but then, unfortunately, a few year years down the road like a good many marriages do, it stops working and then in the split up I sue you for divorce, demanding half of everything you have. It just isn't fair.

LEONARD. Okay, so then don't sue me for half of everything I have.

MYRA. Come on, Leonard, I'm only human. But this way, with the pre-nup in place you haven't got a thing to worry about. You not only get marriage and all the sex you want, you get it with a clear and free mind. It's another win-win situation.

UNCLE FRED. You're a very lucky man. My niece is a very special young lady.

LEONARD. Your niece is a friggen' lunatic.

MYRA. Be patient, Leonard. One day you'll thank me for this.

(Indicates table)

Here, Uncle Fred. We can work at this table.

*(**UNCLE FRED** takes off his jacket, opens his attaché case, takes out a yellow legal pad of paper and pen and sits,*

ready to commence.)

UNCLE FRED. We'll start first by listing your assets…

MYRA. Maybe you can bring out some cookies or something Leonard. It might be a long night.

*(**LEONARD** looks at her in disbelief, then at **UNCLE FRED**. He is not at all sure what his next move is.)*

(BLACK OUT)

Scene 5

TIME: *The next morning.*

The stage is dark. A phone rings. Leonard's dinning room area lights up. **LEONARD**, *in the middle of dressing for work, enters from bedroom and picks up the phone. He is definitely out of sorts.*

LEONARD. Yes!

(Downstage Left, Myra's area LIGHTS UP. She is in bathrobe and slippers and on the phone.)

MYRA. Leonard, I think I owe you an apology.

*(***LEONARD** *hangs up and exits to bedroom.* **MYRA** *dials again.* **LEONARD** *re-enters and picks up the phone.)*

LEONARD. If it's you again I'm going to just continue hanging up.

MYRA. Please, Leonard. Just listen to what I have to say.

LEONARD. No.

MYRA. Look, I need to talk to you. If the only way I can do it is to come over there then I will.

LEONARD. What you and that crazy uncle of yours did last night was insane.

MYRA. I know. I know. Even I think he went a little too far. What was it that pushed it over the edge, my getting your health club membership or dividing up your furniture?

LEONARD. I'm getting sick just thinking about it.

MYRA. Oh, come on, Leonard. Try to understand. He's my uncle. He was simply looking out for me.

LEONARD. I only understand that you and every member of your family that I've met so far are the sickest people I've ever come across in my entire life.

MYRA. Leonard, let's look at the positive side of this. Do you realize half the battle is over? How many couples have worked out a prenup this early in their relationship? You'd be foolish to give up on me now.

LEONARD. First of all, we do not have a relationship. Second of all, that whole prenuptial stuff was stupid, stupid, stupid. We know each other less than a day.

MYRA. If you didn't want to continue the evening, why didn't you say something?

LEONARD. I did, remember? I said "I want the two of you out of here, or I'm calling the police."

MYRA. You did? I must have been in the kitchen taking an inventory when you said that. So why didn't you call the police?

LEONARD. Because your crazy uncle pulled out a gun and said if I tried it he'd shoot me.

MYRA. And you believed him? You are so naive, Leonard, which is one of your greater charms. I swear, you'll soon find that Uncle Fred is the sweetest, kindest and most harmless man in the world. Had I brought Uncle Ralphy with me it would have been a whole different story. Then we'd be talking mob connections, jail time and bodies in the East River. I'll try to put off that meeting as long as I can.

LEONARD. Myra, I think we've talked long enough.

MYRA. You're upset about the sex thing, aren't you? I'll bet that's it.

LEONARD. What sex thing?

MYRA. The fact that we didn't have it. But be reasonable, Leonard, it was getting late and we both had a long night. God, listen to me. I'm making excuses for not having sex. It sounds like we're already married. Somehow I like the feeling. How about you?

LEONARD. You're a very troubled woman, Myra.

MYRA. Of course I am. But I'm doing something about it. I see a therapist three times a week.

LEONARD. Really? The fact that he hasn't had you locked up by now seems to indicate he's not a very good one.

MYRA. First of all, he is a she, and she's amazing. When I started going to her I was a real nothing, Leonard. I was a person without any self confidence, without any self esteem and in less than ten years she's turned me into a totally different person.

LEONARD. How awful. You can probably have her license revoked for that.

MYRA. Well, people who knew me then and know me now feel it was a minor miracle. God, what she could do for you, Leonard. You'd be amazed. As a matter of fact, that isn't a bad idea. I honestly feel if you would see her just a few times, you and I would be in a much better place.

LEONARD. Myra, I want you to take this personally. The only place I can see you right now is in a high security mental ward. Please, don't call here again.

(**LEONARD** *hangs up. His area goes black.*)

MYRA. Why am I always attracted to the needy ones.

(*BLACK OUT*)

Scene 6

TIME: *That evening.*

PLACE: *Leonard's apartment. There is a knock at the door.* **LEONARD** *comes out of the kitchen eating a sandwich.* **LEONARD** *crosses to the door and opens it. It's* **MYRA** *and her therapist,* **GLORIA***.*

LEONARD. Oh, no.

(**LEONARD** *tries closing the door on them.*)

MYRA. Oh, come on, Leonard. Grow up.

(**MYRA** *pushes the door open, and she and* **GLORIA** *enter.*)

LEONARD. I can't believe this! Do I need to get a restraining order, because I'll get one.

MYRA. Leonard, I want you to meet my therapist, Gloria Fossberg.

(**GLORIA** *looks over* **LEONARD***, unimpressed.*)

GLORIA. *(Disappointed)* This is him? This is the man of your dreams? This is who you want to live with the rest of your life, have his babies, cook his meals? God, Myra, I thought we had come a lot farther than this.

LEONARD. Why? What's wrong with me?

GLORIA. Are we on the clock?

MYRA. Yes, of course.

LEONARD. Wait a minute…

MYRA. Don't worry, Leonard. Trust me. It'll be worth every cent.

(**GLORIA** *throws her handbag on the table.*)

GLORIA. Leonard, have you ever gone to a therapist before?

LEONARD. Yes, several times. Once when I was six for unusual thumb sucking and once when I was eighteen for the same thing. I have very little faith in the process.

GLORIA. You hated your mother, didn't you, Leonard?

LEONARD. No, I loved her.

GLORIA. You hated your father then, didn't you?

LEONARD. No, I loved him too.

GLORIA. Leonard, if you're going to fight me on this we're not going to get anywhere. Rule of thumb, everybody hates at least one parent.

LEONARD. Right now I think I hate yours.

MYRA. Please, Leonard, try to co-operate. If you won't do it for yourself, do it for me.

LEONARD. First of all, everything I told her is true. I loved my father, I loved my mother and if you don't believe me, I'll call them and you can ask them yourself.

MYRA. *(A beat)* You mean they're still alive?

LEONARD. Yes, they're still alive.

MYRA. How disappointing.

LEONARD. What do you mean by that?

MYRA. The fact that you've been lying to me about them, there's something very dark, almost sinister about that. As if you're trying to avoid something.

LEONARD. I am. You!

GLORIA. Leonard, you have to understand where Myra's coming from. Because she's undergone as much therapy as she has, she can now easily spot the difficulties and stumbling blocks in front of others. If your parents were dead, where they might not be able to harm you any longer, I could probably have your problems all cleared up in a couple of weeks. But their being alive, that's a whole new deck of cards. I'll have to see you, I'll have to see them. Oh, by the way, I'm a hundred and forty an hour.

MYRA. And well worth it. If you only knew what a bag of trouble I was before I began seeing her, you wouldn't believe it.

GLORIA. I'll attest to that. She's a different girl now, Leonard. Her suicidal tendencies have been dealt with, her lesbian tendencies have been cleared up, her bouts with depression don't last half as long.

LEONARD. Wait a minute. Are you sure as a therapist you should be telling me all this about her?

GLORIA. I'm not speaking as a therapist. I'm speaking as her cousin.

LEONARD. You're her cousin?

MYRA. Her mother and my mother are sisters. I get a twenty percent family discount. Talk about luck.

GLORIA. And the good news, Leonard, is that you also will be entitled to that discount once we can overcome and correct the few, but detrimental obstacles standing in the way of both of you happily walking off, arm in arm into the sunset, as our obvious goal will be.

(Takes out pad and pen from her hand bag and sits on sofa)

Okay, what problem area should we attack first? By any chance are you still sucking your thumb?

LEONARD. No! Of course not.

GLORIA. Good. We can cross homosexuality off the list right now.

MYRA. Didn't I tell you she was great? I'll see you two in a little while.

LEONARD. Wait a minute. Where are you going?

MYRA. I saw a grocery store a couple blocks away. I thought I'd pick up some dinner for us. To tell you the truth, Leonard, I don't really feel like going out tonight. Be good, sweetie.

(She kisses him on the cheek and leaves)

LEONARD. I don't believe this is happening to me.

GLORIA. You're very fortunate. It's so very rare that a person like yourself can connect to someone as remarkable as Myra and finally have commitment make sense. Now then, Leonard, at what age did you first see your mother naked?

(BLACKOUT)

Scene 7

TIME: The next evening.

LIGHTS UP on **LEONARD** *in his apartment and* **MYRA**
in her area. They are both on the phone. **LEONARD** *is
upset.*

MYRA. How much did you say her bill was?

LEONARD. Eight hundred and eighty five dollars.

MYRA. Well, let's figure it out. She came at seven and left at
eleven so that was four hours at one forty an hour. So
one forty and one forty are two eighty and two eighty
and two eighty are five sixty. Okay so far I've got no
problem with that.

LEONARD. No, you don't because you didn't get her bill
which I found slipped under my door when I came
home from work this evening. I almost had a heart
attack when I opened it. And what about that transpor-
tation charge? Three hundred and twenty-five dollars?
Where the hell did that come from.

MYRA. Oh, that was probably for the limo service.

LEONARD. What limo service?

MYRA. Well, you know what it's like trying to catch a cab in
this town. It seemed like a smart move.

LEONARD. Three hundred and twenty-five dollars for limo
service?

MYRA. Leonard, she was there for four hours. There's a waiting charge and then he had to drive us back home.

LEONARD. Look, I don't mind paying her for one hour, I
wouldn't even mind paying her for two hours, but we
didn't talk more than twenty minutes and then she had
to watch a couple of her programs on TV. And then
when you came back from the grocery you invited her
for dinner…

MYRA. It was the polite thing to do, Leonard. After all, she
is my cousin, remember? I don't see the big problem.

LEONARD. The big problem is, I'm getting screwed and not the way I was promised.

MYRA. Well, maybe you can work out some guidelines in the next visit. I think she said she was planning to come over next Wednesday.

LEONARD. There is no next visit. She's sicker than you. She's billing me for almost nine hundred dollars and I know more about her than she knows about me. To hear her scream and carry on all night about her husband, what a low life, cheating son-of-a-bitch he was...

MYRA. That marriage was rocky from the start. Here she waits seven years for a man to get out of jail and two weeks after they marry he's out robbing banks again. It's so stupid. He's eventually going to be caught and there goes another seven years. Poor thing.

LEONARD. Well, I'm not paying her one red cent.

MYRA. It's your choice Leonard but I'm afraid if you don't, it could be a visit from Uncle Ralphy, who also happens to be her father and I don't think it will end up being a pretty picture. By the way, you owe me a hundred and twelve dollars for the groceries.

LEONARD. Why so much? All we had was pasta.

MYRA. I know. I was going to make chicken but after buying the eighty-five dollar bottle of wine, I didn't want to go too crazy.

LEONARD. You need to be stopped, do you know that? You need to be thrown off the top of the Empire State building or put into a space rocket and shot off to another galaxy never to be heard from again because it is wrong for someone like you to remain alive in this once pleasant world.

MYRA. Stop it, right now, Leonard! I am sick and tired of you blaming me for everything. Let's take this thing from the beginning. Who called who?

LEONARD. Okay, okay. I called you. I admit that.

MYRA. But why did you call me? Don't answer that, I will. You called me because you were going nowhere with your life. You called me because you were lonely. Well, guess what? The last two days you haven't been lonely, so stop looking at the negative and start looking at the positive.

LEONARD. You're right. I positively do not want to see you again.

MYRA. Leonard for once in this relationship try and be reasonable.

LEONARD. This is not a relationship.

MYRA. Fine. That's your opinion and you're entitled to it. I see things a little differently. Okay, I will admit that I have behaved unusually aggressive. That I have bamboozled you, overwhelmed your mental circuit board and pushed you into corners that no one deserves to be pushed in to. So why, you ask yourself, did I do this?

LEONARD. Actually, I didn't ask myself anything because I don't care.

MYRA. Well, I'll tell you why? Put yourself in my place, Leonard. I let the last three relationships I had go down the drain because I was not aggressive enough. I let the three biggest loves of my life slip through my fingers because I was a timid little mouse. Three wonderfully bright, well groomed men lost because I was afraid to stake my claim, to assert my position, to declare what's mine is mine. Well, that kind of behavior is over for me, Leonard. With you, I made up my mind that it was going to be different. I've decided to draw a line in the sand and this time people cross it at their own risk.

LEONARD. *(A beat)* Let me get this straight. You actually had three boyfriends?

MYRA. The most wonderful men a girl could ever hope to meet.

LEONARD. And they were in love with you?

MYRA. Madly.

LEONARD. So what happened?

MYRA. Well, the first guy ran off with the second guy and the third guy just disappeared off the face of the earth.

LEONARD. *(A beat)* Myra, at any time while you were dating them, did any of them try holding a pillow over your face.

MYRA. What I'm asking you for, Leonard, is to give us some time. Don't be so eager to rush to judgment. It could be the biggest mistake you'll ever make.

LEONARD. I assure you, it is not a rush to judgment, Myra. It's a fucking desperate dash.

MYRA. Leonard, I did not come to this relationship empty handed. I bring a lot of assets.

LEONARD. Name one.

MYRA. I'm a virgin.

LEONARD. You just said you had three boyfriends.

MYRA. Yes, but we had sex so seldom it hardly counts. I'm also very presentable. I have a very nice wardrobe. You won't be ashamed to take me anywhere.

LEONARD. *(Suspicious)* Okay, what are you getting at now?

MYRA. I saw that you had two tickets for *Jersey Boys* for this Thursday.

LEONARD. How the hell did you see that? I kept them in my underwear drawer.

MYRA. When you were working out the prenuptial with Uncle Fred, I was kind of browsing around. I wanted to find out more about you, the kind of man you are. We live in a very frightening world. You can never know enough about a person. One day you'll have to explain to me what you're doing with a Speedo bathing suit. It can't be a pretty sight. Anyway, back to the tickets for *Jersey Boys*, a show I'm dying to see. And you have such wonderful seats, first row balcony.

LEONARD. I sent away for them last year. I was sure I'd have someone to take by then.

MYRA. And you do, me.

LEONARD. Forget it. I'd rather throw the extra ticket in the river.

MYRA. I'll buy it from you.

LEONARD. It's not for sale.

MYRA. I'll pay you double what you paid for it.

LEONARD. Forget it.

MYRA. You're closing the door on us, aren't you, Leonard?

LEONARD. Not just closing it, Myra. Slamming it shut with a lock, a dead bolt and a chair against the door knob.

MYRA. Just like that.

LEONARD. Exactly like that.

MYRA. You hate me that much.

LEONARD. I don't hate you. I just don't like you.

MYRA. So what I'm hearing is there's still hope.

LEONARD. There is no hope, Myra. None, zero.

MYRA. Okay, Leonard, I see that you're very serious about this, so I'm going to respect your wishes.

LEONARD. That's very decent of you, Myra.

MYRA. You don't want to see me anymore, I understand. These kind of relationships very rarely work out anyway. Where it's all one sided.

LEONARD. That's so true.

MYRA. Just one thing, Leonard, and you can say no if you want to, but is it okay, if we...well, if we can't be lovers, can we maybe just be friends?

LEONARD. No! I'm glad you said I can say that.

MYRA. I'm just talking about an occasional walk in park, maybe a lunch once in awhile, just so we don't lose touch.

LEONARD. I want to loose touch. I'm praying we loose touch.

MYRA. Leonard, I'm bleeding. I need to take something with me from this experience besides a broken heart and crumbled dreams.

LEONARD. I'll send you that Speedo bathing suit. You've ruined that for me too.

MYRA. So what you're saying is we can't be friends.

LEONARD. Absolutely not. At this point I'm not even sure I

can live in the same city with you.

MYRA. Okay, Leonard, then there's something else you need to know about me. I have a stalking problem.

LEONARD. Oh, shit!

MYRA. I didn't want to upset you but that's another reason I'm in therapy. That's why I think we should remain friends. In the long run it's a much easier way out for you.

LEONARD. You're a stalker?

MYRA. I'm afraid that's why my third boyfriend disappeared. I hounded the poor guy to death. I think finding me in his shower with a letter opener in my hand was the final deal breaker.

LEONARD. Oh, my god.

MYRA. Friendship is a much wiser and safer way to go with me, Leonard.

LEONARD. Okay, okay. You convinced me. We'll be friends.

MYRA. You mean that? You're not just saying that?

LEONARD. I don't know why I'm asking you this, Myra, but how can you tell when you're having a stroke?

MYRA. Okay, you want to be friends? I can live with that. I'm not saying it's not disappointing, but it's better than nothing. At least I have a friend. A fine, decent, wonderful friend. I'm starting to feel better again.

LEONARD. I'm happy for you. Now I need to swallow a bottle of Advil so I'm going to say good night.

MYRA. I understand. Good night, friend.

LEONARD. Good night, Myra.

MYRA. No, no. Say it the way I said it. Good night, friend.

LEONARD. Good night, friend.

MYRA. Oh, before I forget, friend. Those two tickets for *Jersey Boys.*

LEONARD. *(Alarmed)* What about them?

MYRA. Well, I know how guys have a habit of losing things and assuming you and I would be an item by Thursday, I took them for safe keeping.

LEONARD. Oh, shit.

MYRA. No, don't worry. It's going to work out okay. I'll meet you in front of the theater Thursday night and give them to you. And please, Leonard, don't feel obligated to take me. After all, we're only friends.

(MYRA *hangs up, satisfied.* LEONARD *hangs up confused.*)

LEONARD. I'm not taking her. No sir, there's no way that woman is going into the theater with me.

BLACKOUT

Scene 8

TIME: Mid afternoon, several weeks later.

PLACE: Leonard's apartment.

Leonard's living room. No one is there. The door bell rings. **NURSE SYLVIA***, wearing her whites and nurse's cap ENTERS from the bedroom and opens the door. It's* **MYRA***. She has a flower pot with only dirt.*

NURSE SYLVIA. Hello.

MYRA. Hi. I'm Myra Witzer.

NURSE SYLVIA. Oh. Oh, I'm sorry but I'm not supposed to let you in.

*(***MYRA*** manages to enter anyway.)*

MYRA. Please, I need to see him. How's he doing?

NURSE SYLVIA. Every day a little bit better.

MYRA. They wouldn't let me in the hospital.

NURSE SYLVIA. Yes. Well, those were his instructions to the doctor in the operating room before they put him under.

MYRA. It made me feel just awful.

NURSE SYLVIA. Well, from what I know about the situation that could have been his intention.

MYRA. It was just such a horrible accident.

NURSE SYLVIA. Yes, yes, it was.

MYRA. I'm just amazed people don't fall off theater balcony's more often. That's the trouble with first row balcony seats, they're quite dangerous. You'd think under the circumstances they'd sell those seats a lot cheaper.

NURSE SYLVIA. You would think so.

MYRA. Maybe I'll write a letter to the *Times*. Poor, Leonard. It was such a shock. One minute he was leaning over the balcony yelling, "There's Al Pacino," and the next minute he was gone.

(The bedroom door opens and **LEONARD***, in pajamas and slippers enters. His head is bandaged, one arm is in*

a sling and he uses a crutch with the other arm.)

LEONARD. Who was at the…

(Spots **MYRA***)*

Oh, no.

(To **NURSE SYLVIA***)*

I specifically told you she wasn't allowed in here.

NURSE SYLVIA. Well, I wasn't going to let her in but she sort of pushed her self in.

LEONARD. Push, push. The way she pushed me off the balcony.

MYRA. Please, Leonard. I did not push you off the balcony. It was the end of act one, I needed to go to the bathroom badly and you were blocking the way. I tried to scoot behind you and well, it didn't work out.

(To **NURSE SYLVIA***)*

I tell you, in a New York theater if you don't get to the ladies room fast, you have to wait forever. They really have to do something about that situation. Maybe I'll mention that too in my letter to the Times.

(To **LEONARD***)*

Anyway, Leonard, you didn't miss anything. The actors were so unnerved by your accident, their timing was off and the second act didn't seem to work as well as the first.

LEONARD. You stayed for the second act? I was lying in a coma and you went back for the second act?

MYRA. Well, there wasn't much to do for you. A couple of ushers carried you to the lobby and we were told that because of the traffic it would be at least an hour for the ambulance. I knew if you lived you'd want to know how the play ended. I mean I wasn't worried that you wouldn't live but with the substandard conditions of the hospitals and the doctors all being unhappy about insurance payments, you never know what could happen. I've been telling people for years, if you don't have to go to the hospital, don't go. Anyway, I'm happy to say you're looking much better than the Edelmans.

LEONARD. The who?

MYRA. The Edelmans. The couple you fell on. They're just beginning to feel sensations in their feet and the wife is almost able to speak whole sentences.

LEONARD. Please go home, Myra. I'll get in touch with you in six or seven years when I'm feeling better.

MYRA. I beg you, Leonard, don't make me feel any worse than I do. By the way, that wasn't Al Pacino you saw. I checked it out. He was in France at the time attending a film festival.

(Holds out flower pot)

Oh, this is for you. I didn't think you were into flowers so I got this instead. If you water it every day in two months you'll have all the oregano you'll ever need.

NURSE SYLVIA. *(Taking flower pot)* Let me take that. I'll put it on the window sill in his bedroom.

MYRA. Thank you.

LEONARD. Put it on the outside ledge. Maybe when she leaves the building it will fall on her head.

*(**NURSE SYLVIA** takes the flower pot and goes into the bedroom with it. **MYRA** sits on the sofa and pats a place for **LEONARD** to sit next to her.)*

MYRA. So, Leonard, long time no see. Why don't you sit down.

LEONARD. Why don't you go home.

MYRA. Look, I understand your anger but keep in mind you have a lot of drugs in your body and they're probably making you a little bit edgier than you already are. So let me start out with some good news. Uncle Fred has agreed to handle your case and thinks you can really clean up.

LEONARD. What are you talking about?

MYRA. Well, since he's going to represent the Edelmans, he thought he might as well represent you too.

LEONARD. He represents the Edelmans?

MYRA. Yes. He contacted them as soon as he learned about the accident on the news. That's how lawyers work. He says they have a real good case. You see you have a case just against the theater, but they have a case against the theater and you.

LEONARD. They're suing me?

MYRA. Yes, but Uncle Fred thinks it's going to be an out of court thing and you shouldn't worry about it. He says with what he thinks he can get for you from the theater you'll still be well ahead of the game. And you'll have an extra benefit because he's giving you the usual family discount which the Edelmans aren't getting.

(LEONARD *starts to cry.* MYRA *gets up to comfort him.*)

Leonard, honey. What's wrong?

LEONARD. I just want you out of my life.

MYRA. Oh, grow up, Leonard. You had an accident. Accidents happen to everybody.

LEONARD. They never happened to me until you showed up. Why are you here, Myra?

MYRA. Leonard, do you remember the last thing I said to you.

LEONARD. Yes. It was "ooops."

MYRA. No, that was when you went over the balcony. I'm talking about when they were wheeling you on the gurney to the ambulance. I'll refresh your memory. I said that I've accepted the fact that you're not marriage material and that I would be looking elsewhere.

LEONARD. Really? You said that? That's wonderful. I'll bet that's why I pulled through the operation.

MYRA. Well, it seems my looking around for someone else at this time is not a good idea.

LEONARD. Why not? I think it's a great idea.

MYRA. Well, I haven't told you everything. I think...I think I screwed up, Leonard.

LEONARD. Now what?

MYRA. Well, you see, while you were lying in sort of a semi-coma in the theater lobby you kept mumbling about your life being a total nightmare.

LEONARD. Which is true ever since you've been in it.

MYRA. Well, the theater manager said to me that it sounded like you were very, very depressed.

LEONARD. Yes. You have that affect on people.

MYRA. Well, foolishly I admitted that you were. That your life was totally unmanageable and that you seemed to be sliding downhill at a breakneck speed.

LEONARD. So?

MYRA. Well, because of that information, the theater is now claiming that your falling off the balcony was a suicide attempt.

LEONARD. That's crazy.

MYRA. Isn't it? Anyway, to cover their settlement with the Edelmans and possibly make a few bucks for themselves, they're countersuing you.

LEONARD. That's more than crazy.

MYRA. Isn't it? But Uncle Fred says they have a great case and instead of you walking away with several hundred thousand dollars for the injuries and hardships you suffered, it's possible the theater will sue you and most likely collect every cent you have to your name.

LEONARD. And you caused all this?

MYRA. I'm afraid I did. And if they make me take the stand, I'm afraid, Leonard, I'd have to tell the truth.

LEONARD. Which is?

MYRA. You've been extremely depressed ever since I've known you.

LEONARD. And you're going to testify to that?

MYRA. I'd be under oath, Leonard. I'd have no choice.

(**LEONARD** *looks at her, nods and begins crying again.*)

LEONARD. I'm screwed.

MYRA. More or less.

LEONARD. Wiped out, ruined.

MYRA. It's basically a case of what can go wrong, usually will.

LEONARD. Finished with a capital F.

MYRA. Among other words. Of course there is one way out.

LEONARD. And that is?

MYRA. Uncle Fred said if we were married, by law I could not legally be forced to testify against you.

LEONARD. *(A beat as it sinks in)* I need to die. I need to be hit by lightning. A huge meteor falling on my head will be okay too.

MYRA. Stop it, Leonard. Now I'll have to testify about that too. Anyway, there is a bright side to all this.

LEONARD. *(Hopeful)* I have cancer and only two hours to live?

MYRA. I have an aunt who's a minister of a lesbian church and has agreed to marry us this weekend.

(**LEONARD** *begins to cry again.*)

Oh, come on, Leonard. It's not that bad. Right after the trial if you want, we can have the marriage annulled. See, Leonard, that prenup we worked out came in handy after all.

(**LEONARD** *continues crying.* **MYRA** *rises.*)

Anyway, think it over, Leonard. It makes great sense to me. In the meantime, I'm going to start making out the guest list. I think I'll give everyone a choice of chicken or fish. I have a nephew who's a caterer. I promise you, with the family discount, it won't be too expensive.

(She rises, gives **LEONARD** *a kiss on top of his head.)*

So long, pumpkin. I'll keep you up on things. Oh, by the way, just to give the wedding a little edge, I'm going to let my mother be the flower girl.

(She exits. Leonard's sobs become louder and louder as we...)

(FADE OUT.)

End of Act I

ACT II

Scene 1

TIME: Several months later. Late afternoon.

SET: Leonard's apartment.

LEONARD *is sitting on a chair at the dinning room table. He's depressed. The door bell rings. He goes to the door, opens it. It's* **GLORIA FOSSBERG**, *Myra's therapist and cousin.*

LEONARD. Hi, Gloria. Thank you so much for coming.

GLORIA. *(Entering)* Please, that's my job. By the way, on house calls, the clock starts when I leave my office.

LEONARD. Fine.

GLORIA. I left two hours ago.

LEONARD. Two hours ago? What did you do, stop off in Wisconsin?

GLORIA. My office is now in my apartment in Westchester. Thanks to you, I discovered I do much better financially making house calls. I need to see much fewer patients plus I really enjoy the limo rides.

LEONARD. Great.

GLORIA. Oh, by the way I now charge a hundred and sixty an hour. My accountant feels I need to be putting more money in my IRA. Now, what seems to be the problem? You sounded desperate over the phone.

LEONARD. I was and I am. Gloria, the marriage is not working out.

GLORIA. Of course it isn't. What did you expect? I know Myra's my cousin, but we have to deal with the facts. She trapped you into a marriage you didn't want. I gave it no chance at all right from the get go. That's why I selected the wedding gift I did, so it would make it easier when you start dividing things up. By the way, I never did get a thank you note.

LEONARD. Oh, sorry. We loved it. And yellow is such a unique color for handkerchiefs. It's obvious a lot of thought went into the selection.

GLORIA. Yellow? In the store they looked white. Oh, well, what does it matter now, right? Okay, Leonard, even though you're only an in-law I'm going to try and be as impartial about the situation between you two as I can. Actually, I will probably be more on your side since Myra is no longer a patient.

LEONARD. Yes, I know. I was planning to ask what happened between the two of you.

GLORIA. Well, unfortunately I made the mistake of pointing out that her marriage to you should be proof to all single women that if a "nut job" like her can get a husband anyone can.

LEONARD. I see. I didn't think therapists used expressions like "nut job."

GLORIA. I didn't tell her that as her therapist. I told her that as her cousin. As her therapist I use the term "rationally challenged."

LEONARD. "Nut job" paints a much more accurate picture.

GLORIA. Doesn't it? Anyway, to the problem at hand, which is how do we get you out of this awful marriage, right?

LEONARD. Wrong.

GLORIA. Wrong?

LEONARD. One hundred percent wrong. You see, Gloria, it's true I was not happy about the marriage. If you recall, I was the only one at the wedding dressed in shorts and sneakers. At the dinner I refused to sit at the same table with the bride, and when anyone came up to me and said "congratulations," I gave them the finger.

GLORIA. Is that what you were doing? I thought you had some kind of a tic. By the way, the salmon they served was excellent.

LEONARD. I heard. I had the cooked to death chicken, which was another thing that pissed me off. Anyway, I was not a happy camper. On our honeymoon in the Bahamas, I insisted on separate rooms.

GLORIA. You were definitely making a statement.

LEONARD. When we came back and she moved in with me, I wouldn't let her redecorate the apartment. I wouldn't even let her hang up any pictures of her mother, even though the one of her sound asleep with her face in the jello wasn't bad. I made up my mind to be the worst son-of-a-bitch I could be. When I'd come home every night from work and Myra had dinner waiting for me, I'd eat and never thank her or tell her if I liked it or not. When she tried to talk to me about how my day was I'd just grunt and never answer.

GLORIA. I have to be honest, Leonard. That's not abnormal behavior for most marriages.

LEONARD. Communication between us was practically zero. On weekends I'd sit on the sofa and just watch ball games. If we went to the movies, we went to one I wanted to see. And then one day...

GLORIA. Yes?

LEONARD. And then one day everything changed. Suddenly I found I actually enjoyed coming home from work with someone waiting for me. I began to really appreciate and look forward to having hot dinners every night and someone to talk to, someone to care about the kind of day I had.

GLORIA. Really?

LEONARD. Yes. It was actually comforting to have someone to watch TV with, go to the movies, with. Suddenly I found myself acting nicer, warmer. I'd sit next to her on the sofa, and hold her hand while we watched her favorite show, *America's Most Wanted*, which incidentally we saw your father and husband on.

GLORIA. Yes. They came off looking very well.

LEONARD. Without realizing what I was doing, I began

referring to Myra in endearing terms, like honey, sweetheart and every now and then, sniggy poo. And just as I once hated every minute being around her, I began to hate every minute not being around her.

GLORIA. That's just wonderful, Leonard. So what's the problem?

LEONARD. The problem is...the problem is...

GLORIA. Spit it out, Leonard. The limo is waiting and I need to stop at Bloomingdales.

LEONARD. The problem is, the more I got to like married life, the less she did. The closer I wanted to get to her, the farther she wanted to be from me. Everything between us just seemed to turn topsy turvy. No longer is there a hot meal waiting for me at night. No longer does she sit on the sofa with me and hold hands or go with me to the movies.

GLORIA. My, my, my.

LEONARD. Exactly. Nothing nice I do seems to matter. When I bring home flowers she doesn't even put them in a vase. When I buy her a box of candy, she eats all the good ones before she offers me any. And just recently she's refusing to wash our clothes together.

GLORIA. You poor guy. It has to be hell. Where is she now?

LEONARD. Somewhere in Central Park. She goes there every day and sits on a bench and just thinks.

GLORIA. That can be very dangerous.

LEONARD. I told her that. With all the gang bangers and muggers running around...

GLORIA. I'm referring to the thinking part. Is it possible she has another guy?

LEONARD. I doubt it. How many guys are there in this world with a death wish?

GLORIA. True. What about sex?

LEONARD. What about it?

GLORIA. Is there any?

LEONARD. Well, on our honeymoon there wasn't.

GLORIA. Understandable.

LEONARD. But then on the flight back things changed.

GLORIA. The reason being?

LEONARD. Well, she started telling me about the mile high club. You know, where you have sex in the airplane bathroom.

GLORIA. And?

LEONARD. Well, I'm ashamed to say I tried it with her.

GLORIA. And?

LEONARD. It was awful. Somehow it got so hot and heavy, the smoke detector went off and the plane made an emergency landing in Cleveland.

GLORIA. What a coincidence. That happened to me once.

LEONARD. I didn't like Cleveland. The FBI agents that stripped searched us were very unfriendly. Also, it was winter time and their hands were very cold.

GLORIA. So then there was sex in the marriage.

LEONARD. Oh, yes. Of course at the beginning it was sex for sex sake, no pillow talk, no foreplay, no fake orgasms from either of us. Just bam bam bam and good night.

GLORIA. Once again, very normal behavior for a married couple.

LEONARD. And then as the weeks progressed, the sex became less perfunctory. I found myself wanting to hold her more, to cuddle, to stroke her hair, kiss her lips.

GLORIA. Interesting.

LEONARD. Isn't it? And then like I told you, as things got better, things got worse. As sex continued to be a truly loving, exciting experience for me, it began to turn her off. As I strived for more intimacy at night, she began to talk about twin beds. As I came to bed with less clothes on, she came to bed with more clothes on. Last night she slept with shoes, a rain coat and a baseball bat.

GLORIA. Hmm. Why a raincoat?

LEONARD. That puzzled me too. That's why I need your help, Gloria. I'll do anything to save this marriage. Anything.

(The front door opens and **MYRA** *enters.)*

GLORIA. Ahh, speak of the devil.

LEONARD. Hi, honey. We were just talking about you.

MYRA. Hello, Gloria. I see you rented a stretch limo this time.

LEONARD. *(Annoyed)* A stretch limo? What the hell did you need a stretch limo for?

GLORIA. For another sixty dollars an hour it seemed to make sense.

LEONARD. Honey, I thought that maybe Gloria could help us with our marital problem.

MYRA. Oh?

LEONARD. Yes. I seem to be having trouble with the fact that one of us is not happily married and it isn't me.

GLORIA. I would have bet my ass against a glass of water it would have been the other way around.

MYRA. Unfortunately, Leonard, what we are experiencing is not a problem.

LEONARD. No?

MYRA. No. It's a condition and today I finally decided how I need to deal with it. Leonard, I put in a call to my Uncle Fred. I'm going to have our marriage annulled.

LEONARD. What?

GLORIA. Tough break, Leonard. There goes your family discount.

MYRA. I want out, Leonard.

LEONARD. I don't understand. I'm a totally different person now than the one you married. I've gotten a whole different spin on intimacy and commitment. I'm now loving and caring and considerate. Even my friends have pointed out what a pussy I've turned into.

MYRA. I tricked you into this marriage, Leonard. You didn't have to marry me. I lied about the law suit. The truth is nobody is suing anybody.

LEONARD. The theater is not suing me?

MYRA. No and neither are the Edelmans.

LEONARD. Really? Then why do I keep getting bills from your Uncle Fred? Anyway, it doesn't matter. Trick or not, I love being married to you, Myra. You've brightened my life, filled it with happiness and joy as well as a few other things I haven't yet quite identified.

MYRA. It's not you, Leonard, it's me. This may be difficult for you to understand, but before we got married my every waking minute seemed to be in the pursuit of a husband. I was consumed by the desire to be married. Well, now that I am married, I feel an emptiness. Something is missing in me and I don't know what.

LEONARD. I don't see anything missing, Myra, outside of a better grasp on mental soundness. For some unexplainable reason, you're the perfect person for me.

MYRA. That may be, Leonard, but are you the perfect person for me? Obviously not or why would I feel this way? Anyway, I've decided to move back in with my mother.

LEONARD. And do what?

MYRA. What ever it was I was doing before we got married.

LEONARD. You were looking for a husband.

MYRA. What can I tell you, Leonard? It seemed to do the trick. God, I'm so relieved I got this over with. I actually feel as happy now as when I got you to marry me. I'm going to pack my things.

LEONARD. Just like that?

MYRA. Why prolong pain if you don't have to.

LEONARD. I don't know, but if you give me enough time I'm sure I'll come up with a good reason.

MYRA. *(Stroking his cheek)* Poor, poor, Leonard. You are such a glutton for punishment, aren't you?

(She starts for the bedroom. **LEONARD** *jumps in front of her.)*

LEONARD. Please, Myra. Wait. Here's an idea. Why don't you stay here and I'll move in with your mother. I'll stay there as long as you want. Four months, six months, a year. What ever time it takes for you to get through this...this cobweb of deranged emotions. Then when you come to your senses and realize our marriage wasn't that bad and you want me back, I'm sure my living with your mother will have made me as loony as you are, and we'll be a perfect match.

MYRA. I'm sorry, Leonard. The ship has sailed.

*(**MYRA** EXITS to bedroom and closes the door. **LEONARD** goes to the door and shouts through it.)*

LEONARD. *(Shouting after her)* Hey, that's a good idea. A cruise. Maybe that's what we need. A trip to some romantic and exotic place. I'll find out if there's any where left in the world where they still like Americans and we'll go there. What do you say?

*(He sees it's hopeless. To **GLORIA**)*

Well, thanks for jumping in.

GLORIA. There was no need. The fix is obvious.

LEONARD. Not to me.

GLORIA. That's why you have me. Think about this, Leonard. What was the one thing missing in your early relationship?

LEONARD. Mace?

GLORIA. Keep going.

LEONARD. I'm sticking with mace. Give me the goddamn answer. She's packing.

GLORIA. Courtship! There was no courtship. Women have a need for courtship and if they don't get it before the marriage the problem of not getting it shows up after the marriage.

LEONARD. Courtship? Yeah, you're right. There was no courtship period. She just kind of went after me caveman style, clobbered me over the head and dragged me off.

GLORIA. Exactly. And now she wants you to do that to her.

LEONARD. Well, I do like the clobbering over the head part.

GLORIA. She wants what every woman wants before becoming knotted up in the binding chains of matrimony. She wants to be pursued, Leonard. Swept off her feet. Carried off into the sunset. God, I'm good. Can you imagine what I could have done had I gone to college for this stuff?

LEONARD. You don't have a degree?

GLORIA. What for? What I do is mostly dispense common sense. What works, works. What doesn't, doesn't. You can't get better results than that even with the proper credentials.

LEONARD. So what you're saying is that now Myra wants me to go after her?

GLORIA. Exactly.

LEONARD. What about the annulment?

GLORIA. *(Preparing to leave)* Let her get it. You'll just get married again. On the upside, I'm sure she'll want another wedding and this time you can order the salmon. Sometimes it's amazing how wonderfully things work out. I'll send you my bill.

*(***GLORIA*** EXITS.)*

LEONARD. Damn it, she's expensive, but she's good.

(BLACKOUT)

Scene 2

TIME: Evening.

The set is dark. Lights up on **LEONARD** *dialing his phone. Lights up on Myra's phone. It rings several times.* **MYRA** *ENTERS and picks it up.*

MYRA. Hello.

LEONARD. Hello, Myra. It's me again.

MYRA. Please, Leonard. I told you, you've got to forget me.

LEONARD. I can't. Since you've been gone something is missing. And it's not just the noise in my head. I can't go on. I mope around the apartment all day. I can't concentrate on my work. My life is an absolute misery without you.

MYRA. Leonard, I've only been gone one day.

LEONARD. Is that all? No wonder I'm not better.

MYRA. You've called me at least thirty times. I'm starting to get very, very edgy, as well as a bit fed up.

LEONARD. I'm sorry. Myra, Gloria put this thought in my head and you've got to be truthful with me. Have you found someone else?

MYRA. How could I, Leonard? I've been too busy answering the phone. I haven't even had time to post my availability on the internet.

LEONARD. You're going online? That's awful. All you meet are murderers and rapists and perverts.

MYRA. Well, a girl has to start somewhere.

LEONARD. You're not a girl, Myra. You're a woman.

MYRA. What's on your mind, Leonard? I'm really very busy unpacking.

LEONARD. I want you back, Myra. I can't live without you.

MYRA. Yes, you can.

LEONARD. No, I can't.

MYRA. Yes, you can.

LEONARD. No, I can't.

MYRA. Prove it.

LEONARD. What?

MYRA. Prove it. You said you can't live without me, I said prove it.

LEONARD. That's stupid. The only way to prove it is to kill myself and if I kill myself then you'll never come back to me.

MYRA. So then what's the point you're making?

LEONARD. The point I'm making is that for some weird reason I've fallen in love with you, Myra, and I can't go on without you.

MYRA. Yes, you can.

LEONARD. No, I can't.

MYRA. Yes, you can.

LEONARD. No, I can't.

MYRA. Prove it.

LEONARD. Goddamn it, Myra, if we can't discuss this like two adults then I'm just going to hang up on you and call back in two minutes in hopes you've had time to think a little more clearly about this and come to your senses.

MYRA. Please, Leonard, you've got to let go. I don't want to hurt you any more than I have.

LEONARD. That, Myra, is impossible.

MYRA. Leonard, just what is it about me you liked?

LEONARD. What is it about you I liked?

MYRA. Yes, maybe you might have noticed a couple of nice attributes that I can mention on the internet.

LEONARD. Well, there are a lot of things I like about you, Myra.

MYRA. I need to hear the list, Leonard.

LEONARD. Well, to tell you the truth I never really got to know you that well. At the beginning I was too busy trying to get rid of you and then at the end you were too busy trying to get rid of me.

MYRA. Well if you come up with anything, please give me a call.

LEONARD. Look, Myra, before either of us gives this situation too much thought, I wonder how you would feel about this idea. Since there's no one in either of our lives right now and since you're planning to have our marriage annulled, throwing us back on the open market again, maybe it might be a wise thing for both of us to do some preparatory work.

MYRA. Like what?

LEONARD. Well, like using each other to practice dating.

MYRA. Can I have that again?

LEONARD. We go out together and use each other to brush up on our dating techniques.

MYRA. Leonard, this sounds like a very bad television idea.

LEONARD. So what? If it works that's all that counts. Now let's arrange something that will be like a first date for us. What if we meet somewhere for coffee?

MYRA. I don't drink coffee, Leonard. You know that.

LEONARD. How could I? This will be our first date. Get it?

MYRA. This is stupid.

LEONARD. Let's not be negative. Okay, you don't drink coffee. So how's this? What if we meet at the scene of the original crime, Manny's Deli?

MYRA. You hated our first date there. You had an awful time. You never wanted to see me again after that.

LEONARD. I know. Those were the good old days.

MYRA. Leonard, I'm tired and it's late. Can I have a few days to think about it?

LEONARD. No. The last time you did any thinking, you left me. Just say yes, okay?

MYRA. I don't know…

LEONARD. Please, Myra. I'm on my knees and I'm wearing my good suit pants. Now what about tomorrow night, say at seven?

MYRA. I just think it's too soon, Leonard.

LEONARD. Okay, then we'll make it at eight. How's that.

MYRA. You're not going to stop calling until I say yes.

LEONARD. I don't think so.

MYRA. Okay. Tomorrow night at eight.

LEONARD. You mean it?

MYRA. I mean it.

LEONARD. You've made me the happiest man in the world, Myra.

MYRA. Yes. But you need to know, Leonard, I'm not very comfortable doing that.

(BLACKOUT)

Scene 3

TIME: The next evening.

PLACE: The booth at Manny's Deli.

LEONARD *is sitting by himself. He is a bit impatient. He looks at his watch.* **MYRA** *ENTERS and sits down.*

MYRA. Hello, Leonard.

LEONARD. You're an hour late.

MYRA. I know.

LEONARD. Aren't you going to tell me why?

MYRA. I couldn't find Mother.

LEONARD. Where did she go?

MYRA. Nowhere. She's in her apartment. But sometimes when she's depressed she'll hide.

LEONARD. It's a small two bedroom apartment. Where could she possibly hide?

MYRA. I have no idea, but she's very good at it.

LEONARD. She must be. What was she depressed about?

MYRA. Oh, nothing serious. Some parents just get depressed when their grown children move back in with them.

(Sniffs)

Something smells like...like brine.

LEONARD. That's me. Waiting for you I ate three dishes of dill pickles and a lot of it dripped on my clothes.

MYRA. You need to know up front that I don't want to be here.

LEONARD. Well, you're here and that's all that counts. Want a pickle? There's only one left.

MYRA. No thanks. Let's just get this over with.

LEONARD. Okay, okay. So Myra Witzer, tell me a little about yourself.

MYRA. Why?

LEONARD. Because this is supposed to be our first date, that's why. We need to treat it like that for the evening to work.

MYRA. Okay. A little about myself. Well, I'm thirty-two.

LEONARD. Keep going.

MYRA. Thirty-four.

LEONARD. One more jump.

MYRA. Thirty-eight, and you're a real asshole.

LEONARD. Just trying to keep you honest. Anything else I should know about you?

MYRA. Well, I was recently married but I'm now, thank God, in the process of getting that annulled.

LEONARD. Interesting. You want to talk about it?

MYRA. Not really?

LEONARD. You want to talk about your soon-to-be ex?

MYRA. Not really?

LEONARD. Why not?

MYRA. It's over. He's yesterday's news. Time to move on.

LEONARD. Very harsh.

MYRA. Isn't it.

LEONARD. Strangely enough, I was recently married, and I'm also in the process of getting that annulled.

MYRA. Oh?

LEONARD. Yes. You want to hear about it?

MYRA. No, not really?

LEONARD. You want to hear about my soon-to-be ex?

MYRA. I don't think so?

LEONARD. Goddamn it, Myra, we have to talk about something.

MYRA. Well, think of something besides us. There is no more us. It's over and done with. Isn't that why we're dating?

LEONARD. I wasn't talking about us-us. I was talking about your husband and my wife. Right now that's ex-us not us-us. You and I are a different couple.

MYRA. All right, you want to talk about them, let's talk about them. But all it's going to do is ruin what could be a perfectly mediocre evening.

LEONARD. *(Raising his voice)* Goddamn it, Myra, can't you make an effort to be a little bit positive.

MYRA. Please, Leonard, you're raising your voice.

LEONARD. No, you're raising it. I came here with high hopes, expectations, dreams and what am I getting so far? Heartburn from all the goddamn pickles I ate while waiting for you. Look, I'm trying to save a marriage.

MYRA. Well you're wasting your time.

LEONARD. I refuse to believe that.

MYRA. Look, Leonard. How long were we married?

LEONARD. Three months, seven days, seventeen hours and...

(looks at watch)

...twenty-one minutes.

MYRA. Okay. Now what if we looked at marriage like a bottle of milk. A bottle of milk has an expiration date on it. Sometimes it's a week, sometimes it's a week and a half. It all depends when you buy it, how much time you have to drink it. Sometimes it expires before you finish drinking the milk which apparently is what happened in our case.

LEONARD. That's an amazing analogy, Myra. Amazing. As God as my witness, I will never drink milk again.

MYRA. I'm sorry, Leonard, I can't find a better way to explain it.

(A WAITER ENTERS and approaches booth.)

WAITER. Have you two decided what you wanted to order?

LEONARD. *(To MYRA)* Without going into any long dissertation, Myra, is there any chance that you and I might end up having sex tonight?

MYRA. I doubt it.

LEONARD. *(To WAITER)* Two grilled cheese sandwiches.

WAITER. Any fries with that?

LEONARD. *(To MYRA)* What about a hand job in the cab on the way home?

MYRA. Not a prayer.

LEONARD. No fries.

WAITER. Anything to drink?

LEONARD. Anything but milk.

(The **WAITER** *EXITS.)*

LEONARD *(Cont.)* You would have thought I would have learned my lesson. The first, first time I went out with you, I never wanted to see you again. And now on our second first time I'm starting to feel the exact same way.

MYRA. Well, then be thankful about it.

LEONARD. And the reason I should be?

MYRA. Because it's the best thing for you, Leonard. To leave here so angry that you never want to see me again. That will solve all your problems.

LEONARD. I don't want them solved. I want you. I love you Myra Witzer Shank. Doesn't that mean anything to you?

MYRA. I don't want to hear this, Leonard.

LEONARD. Well, maybe you should. You can't do this to me, Myra. Make me fall in love with you and then dump me the way you did.

MYRA. I need to go.

(Rises)

LEONARD. I'm sorry, Myra. I can't help myself.

MYRA. I know. And I do feel terrible about it. That's why it's best I go.

LEONARD. What about your grilled cheese?

MYRA. Put it in the mail.

LEONARD. Can I call you later tonight?

MYRA. No.

LEONARD. Okay, then what about a second date?

MYRA. You are exhausting me to a very dangerous level. Leonard, try to understand. I don't want to hurt you. What's happening is not your fault, it's mine. Isn't it possible to just part friends.

LEONARD. No! We've been married too long for that.

MYRA. Goodbye, Leonard.

LEONARD. No, no, wait. My back's against the wall. I know this evening didn't go well, whether it was my fault or... my fault. But I'll make a deal with you, Myra. I need to take one last shot at it.

MYRA. I think this was it.

LEONARD. No, please, this was a practice last shot, remember. Next time I promise will be my real last shot. If next time it doesn't work I promise we'll call it a day and you'll never hear from me again, ever.

MYRA. You mean it?

LEONARD. I swear.

MYRA. Okay, what's the plan this time.

LEONARD. I'm going to get two more tickets for *Jersey Boys,* and I want you to see it with me.

MYRA. I already saw it with you.

LEONARD. Yes. But only the first act if you recall.

MYRA. I swear, Leonard, your falling off the balcony was an accident.

LEONARD. Yes, yes. I believe that. But here's my reasoning. Despite the fact that I only got to see the first act, no show ever left me feeling as excited, as uplifted, as happy to be there as that one. How about you?

MYRA. Well, yes, I felt that way too. So?

LEONARD. So, I think it could be the perfect venue to start things up for us again. I have a strong feeling that sitting through that wonderful musical experience, we'll once again enjoy being together, once again hold hands, squeeze fingers, once again feel the magic in our hearts. At a hundred and ten bucks a ticket, I don't think I'm asking for too much.

MYRA. Frankly, I think you're asking for a miracle.

LEONARD. Maybe. But if miracles can't happen in the theater, then just where the hell can they happen? Please,

Myra. Please.

MYRA. *(Sighs)* Okay, Leonard. But this is it. The last chance, you promise?

LEONARD. I promise.

MYRA. Okay. Call me when you get the tickets. I need to go home now and look for my mother.

LEONARD. Wait. Would it be okay if I kissed you good night?

MYRA. I'm sorry, Leonard. Not on the first date.

(She exits. LEONARD sits down and sighs.)

LEONARD. *Jersey Boys,* it's all up to you.

(BLACKOUT)

Scene 4

TIME: *Several years later. A Spring afternoon.*

PLACE: *A park bench.*

Downstage Center has afternoon lighting. **MYRA** *is on the bench reading a book.* **LEONARD** *comes by wheeling a stroller. He is wearing sunglasses. As he passes* **MYRA***, he stops and looks back at her.*

LEONARD. Myra!

(**MYRA** *looks up. She doesn't recognize him.*)

MYRA. Yes?

LEONARD. It's me. Leonard.

MYRA. *(It hasn't sunk in yet)* Leonard?

LEONARD. Leonard. Leonard Shank.

(*He removes his sun glasses*)

We were married once.

MYRA. *(Now it sinks in)* Oh, Leonard. Yes, of course, Leonard. I didn't recognize you with those sunglasses. How are you Leonard?

LEONARD. I'm fine. I'm fine. And you?

MYRA. Also fine.

LEONARD. How nice. Gosh, it's been a long time. Five almost six years.

MYRA. Yes, that's about right.

(*Indicates stroller*)

Is that a baby in there?

LEONARD. Yes. My son. Robert. He's eight months old.

MYRA. Oh, how wonderful. In New York you can never be sure what's in a stroller. Dogs, cats. People are so weird with their pets.

LEONARD. Well, that's a real person in there. Robert Wong Shank.

MYRA. Wong?

LEONARD. It's my wife's maiden name. She's Asian.

MYRA. So you remarried?

LEONARD. Yes. About two years ago.

MYRA. How nice.

LEONARD. Yes. I met her at a singles dance. She spoke no English. It's made life so much easier. And you?

(Sits next to her)

MYRA. No. I've come close several times but when push came to shove, well it never seemed to work out. Speaking of shove, I assume everything's healed since that last unfortunate incident.

LEONARD. You mean my second fall from the theater balcony?

MYRA. Yes. *Jersey Boys* was not a lucky show for you.

LEONARD. Seems that way.

MYRA. What's funny, if you can call it that, is that this time it really was Al Pacino you saw.

LEONARD. I know. Nice guy. He came to visit me in the hospital.

MYRA. Really?

LEONARD. The bigger they are the nicer they are. He even brought me a box of candy. I was hoping you'd come to visit.

MYRA. Well, I didn't want to upset you. I remembered how angry you were at me the first time you fell over.

LEONARD. Well, accidents happen.

MYRA. I know, but this time it really wasn't an accident. I pushed you over, remember? I just couldn't help myself, Leonard. Those phone calls from you at all hours of the night, I was sleep deprived. People do crazy things when they're sleep deprived. I had to get rid of you.

LEONARD. I know. And I don't blame you one bit. I was out of control.

MYRA. It was so nice of you not to press charges.

LEONARD. Well, when they were wheeling me into the

emergency room I had a chance to really think things through. I realized I had driven you to it. As soon as I got out of the hospital I checked myself into rehab. They have a whole program for people with broken hearts.

MYRA. How nice.

LEONARD. Yeah. It works great. I was totally over you in two years, four months and seventeen days.

MYRA. Good for you. And there were no further complications from the balcony fall?

LEONARD. Well, yes and no. I still suffer from a serious fear of heights, but my therapist said eventually that will go away too, the way my limp and stuttering did.

MYRA. Oh, good.

LEONARD. Nowadays very few people go through life without a problem or two.

MYRA. Isn't that the truth.

LEONARD. Are you still living with your mother?

MYRA. No, she's been gone now for three years.

LEONARD. Oh, I'm sorry. She was a wonderful person. A very good eater as I remember. You must miss her terribly?

MYRA. Oh, she didn't die. I had to put her in a home.

LEONARD. Oh, that's too bad.

MYRA. The neighbors kept complaining about her saxophone playing.

LEONARD. She played the saxophone? I didn't know that.

MYRA. Yes. Quite honestly, she was never really good at it. The neighbors had every right to complain. What time do you have? I left my watch at home.

LEONARD. It's almost one.

MYRA. I'm on my lunch hour. I have this wonderful job I really love.

LEONARD. What do you do?

MYRA. I work for the suicide hot line. I answer phones. I get to talk to some very interesting people.

LEONARD. I'll bet.

MYRA. I've actually dated a few. Never anything serious. They all seemed even more troubled than I am. But you have to keep at it. You never know when Mr. Right is going to show up.

LEONARD. Isn't that the truth.

MYRA. Frankly, I'm not sure I even want to try marriage again. Not everybody needs to be married. I actually kind of like single life. Less pressure put on you to be reasonable. Although sometimes, on a nice afternoon like today, when I see couples walk by holding hands or even husbands pushing strollers, I sometimes wonder if I'm missing the boat. But then Leonard, I think back to us...

LEONARD. Yes?

MYRA. And I don't think I am. No disrespect intended.

LEONARD. Of course not.

MYRA. *(A beat)* One of my therapists suggested it could just be a hormonal thing with me. But that's going in a whole different direction.

LEONARD. I've given our relationship a great deal of thought too. I think I have you figured out, Myra. It's not really marriage that interests you. It's the fun of the hunt.

MYRA. Really?

LEONARD. I definitely think so. You enjoy the challenge of the chase even more than the capture. There are people like that, who, when they've captured their prey feel everything else is anti-climatic.

MYRA. That's very insightful. And what about you?

LEONARD. I seem to enjoy the capture, the imprisonment. There are people like that too.

MYRA. Hmm. I think you could be on to something. Life is so bizarre.

LEONARD. I don't know a better way to describe it.

(Looks at watch)

Well, I'd better be going. It's almost little Robert Wong's feeding time. It was nice bumping into you, Myra.

MYRA. It's was nice seeing you again too, Leonard.

LEONARD. *(Rises)* You know I wonder if when we got together, if we were as insightful as we are now, would it have made any difference?

MYRA. We'll never know, will we?

LEONARD. No, I guess not. We'll never know.

MYRA. But I seriously doubt it.

LEONARD. Good. I think that sort of clears the boards. Myra, would you mind…

MYRA. Yes?

LEONARD. Would you mind if, before I left, I kissed you on the cheek?

MYRA. Do you think it's appropriate?

LEONARD. I don't know if it is or it isn't. It's just something I would like to do.

MYRA. Well, I guess it would be okay. What harm could it do? We never did get to say goodbye officially.

*(**LEONARD** kisses her softly on the cheek. **MYRA** touches her face. She is definitely moved.)*

MYRA. *(Cont.)* That was sweet.

LEONARD. Yes. Yes it was. Very sweet. Goodbye, Myra.

MYRA. Goodbye Leonard.

*(**LEONARD** goes off. **MYRA** watches for a beat, then touches her face once more, sighs and then continues reading. **HOWARD**, a man in his mid-forties comes to the bench and sits next to her.)*

HOWARD. Hi.

MYRA. Hi.

HOWARD. You look familiar.

MYRA. No, I don't.

HOWARD. I think we must have met somewhere.

MYRA. You know we didn't.

HOWARD. I'm really very lonely and I was hoping you were too.

MYRA. Bingo! My name's Myra.

HOWARD. My name's Howard. Maybe you'd like to go out for coffee sometime?

MYRA. That's a possibility. I never liked coffee, but maybe I need to give it another chance. Sometimes you need to give a lot of things you think you don't like another chance.

HOWARD. Isn't that the truth. You seem to be a very interesting woman, Myra.

MYRA. You have no idea.

(The stage dims.)

(CURTAIN)

PROPS

ACT I

Scene 1
2 cordless phones
Small table

Scene 2
3 table settings, a plate of pickles, mustard, ketchup, bread basket with bread and butter

Scene 3
2 cordless phones
Small table

Scene 4
Briefcase
Yellow legal pad of paper
Pen

Scene 5
2 cordless phones
Small table

Scene 6
Large hand bag containing a pen and a pad of paper

Scene 7
2 cordless phones
Small table

Scene 8
Flower pot with only dirt
Crutch
Arm sling

ACT TWO

Scene 2
2 cordless phones
Small table

Scene 3
2 table settings, a plate of pickles, mustard, ketchup, bread basket

Scene 4
Book
Baby stroller, baby blanket, and doll

COSTUMES

ACT I

Scene 1

Leonard - Suit, pants, dress shirt, tie
Myra – Skirt, blouse

Scene 2

Myra – Sweater, skirt, watch
Florence – Dress, sweater
Leonard – Sport coat, slacks, sport shirt

Scene 3

Myra – Same as Scene 2
Leonard – Same as Scene 2

Scene 4

Leonard – Pajamas, slippers, silk robe
Myra – Same as Scene 2 and a light coat
Fred – Suite, shirt, tie

Scene 5

Leonard – Pants, white shirt, untied tie
Myra – Bathrobe, slippers

Scene 6

Leonard – Pants, sweatshirt
Myra – Dress
Gloria – Pant suit, blouse

Scene 7

Leonard – Pants, white shirt
Myra – Skirt, blouse

Scene 8

Nurse Sylvia – Nurse's white uniform and cap
Myra – Dress
Leonard – Pajamas, slippers

ACT II

Scene 1

Leonard – Slacks, shirt, watch
Gloria – Jacket, skirt
Myra – Skirt, sweater

Scene 2

Leonard – Slacks, shirt
Myra – Bathrobe, slippers

Scene 3

Leonard – Slacks, shirt, sweater, watch
Myra – Skirt, blouse
Waiter – Black pants, white shirt, black vest

Scene 4

Myra - Skirt, light jacket
Leonard – Warm-up jacket, shirt, slacks, watch
Howard – Corduroy jacket, shirt, slacks

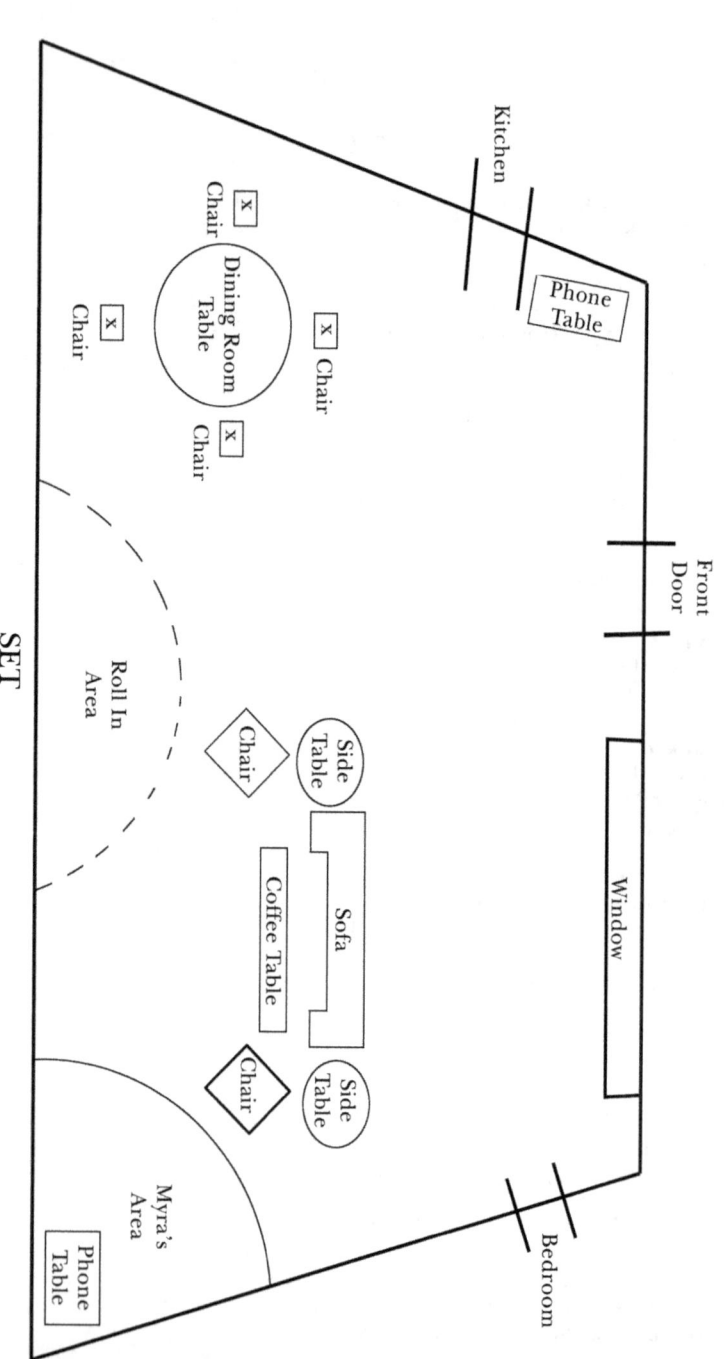

SET

Also by
Sam Bobrick...

Annoyance
Are You Sure?
Baggage
The Crazy Time
Death in England
Flemming (An American Thriller)
Getting Sara Married
Hamlet II (Better Than the Original)
Murder at the Howard Johnson's
New York Water
No Hard Feelings
Norman, Is That You?
The Outrageous Adventures of
Sheldon and Mrs. Levine
Passengers
Remember Me?
Splitting Issues
The Stanway Case
Wally's Cafe
Weekend Comedy